North Island

Northland Forest Park
(Tane Mahuta)

Rotorua
(Volcanoes and geysers)

Wellington
(Capital city)

Kaikoura
(Whales)

Mount Cook
(Highest mountain)

South Island

Thank you

Dad, Mum, Porus, Rebecca, Ethan,Tegan and Zenobia x

First paperback edition published in Great Britain in 2012 by Bustani
244 Franciscan Road, London, SW17 8HF
contact@bustani.co.uk

A CIP catalogue record of this book is available from the British Library.

ISBN 978-0-9573358-0-6

Printed in Great Britain

www.bustani.co.uk

BUDDY
in New Zealand

Nazneen Bustani

This book belongs to
the great explorer

Sage Taylor.

Dearest
Sagie, My
lovely 4 and a ½ year
old lots of love
Dadda!

BUSTANI

BUDDY, the dog, loves adventures.

He was ready for a new one
with best friend Peggy.

Buddy said the magic words...

Kula...

Kulo...

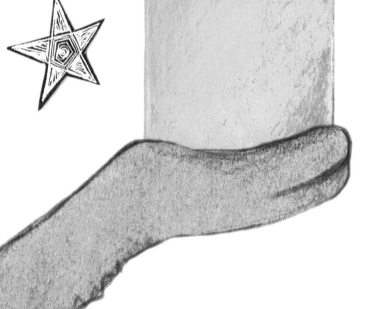

Kulapa...

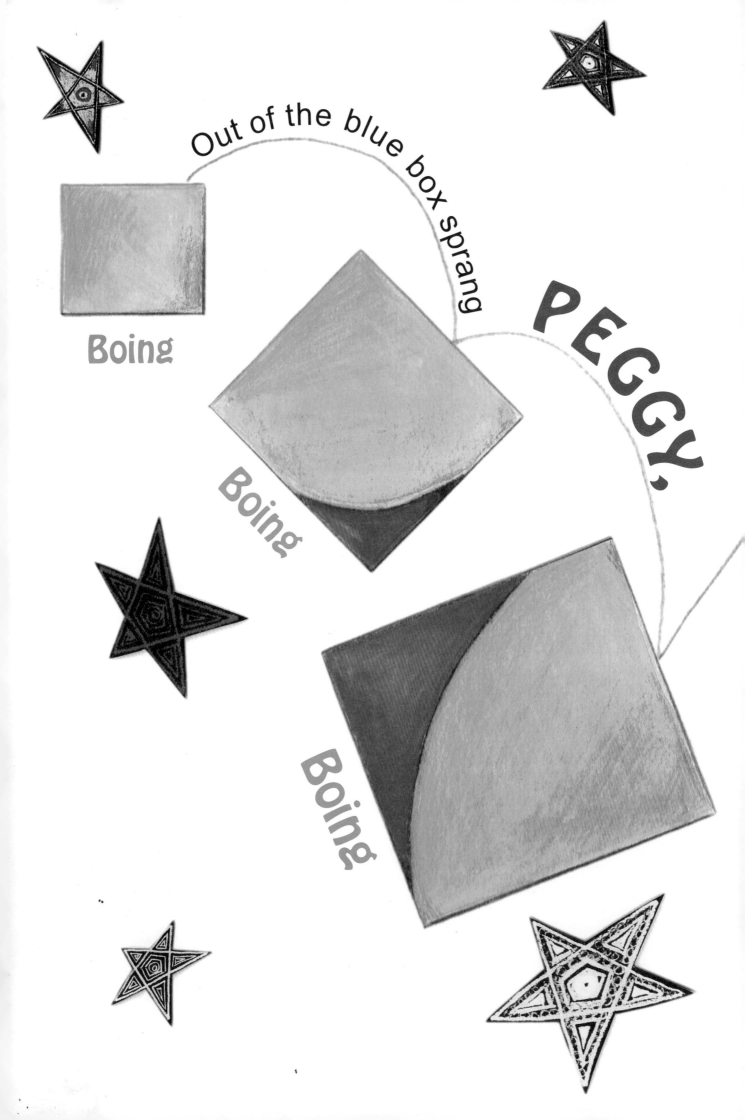

Out of the blue box sprang PEGGY.

Boing

Boing

Boing

the magic tent.

"Wow!" said Peggy. "Where are we?"

"We're in New Zealand.
On top of Mount Cook," replied Buddy.

AVALANCHE

Buddy and Peggy were on the highest mountain in New Zealand. Suddenly Mount Cook rumbled and the ice crumbled. They slid down the slope and just missed the crashing ice.

Uh-oh

Peggy decided to use her flying powers.
They whizzed up South Island till Buddy heard...
"Cheep cheep."
"Look, a lost chick," said Buddy.
"Chukpuk, join us on our adventure."
"Chirpy cheep."

SPLISH

The three adventurers Buddy, Peggy and Chukpuk flew to Kaikoura, where they got soaked by big splashing whales.

Chukpuk also wanted to see the North Island. So they visited Rotorua, a wonderland of volcanoes and geysers. Buddy and Chukpuk had a poptastic time when the geysers spurted gas from holes in the ground.

But Peggy wasn't amused. She felt sick.
"Can we go now?" she moaned.
"This place smells of rotten eggs."

Yuck!

They left Rotorua but Peggy still felt dizzy. Suddenly she stopped flying. "Please help me," cried Peggy.

SPLITTER

SPLATTER

SPLUT

Buddy and Chukpuk ran to get help. But they couldn't find their way in the dense rainforest. "Oh no!" they said. "We're lost!"

After a while, Buddy and Chukpuk bumped into a huge tree. A deep voice said,

Kia ora!
I am Tane Mahuta,
the Lord of the Forest.
I am the oldest and wisest
Kauri tree. We are the mightiest
trees in New Zealand.
Your friend needs medicine
from the Maori people.
The middle path will lead you to
the gateway of their village.

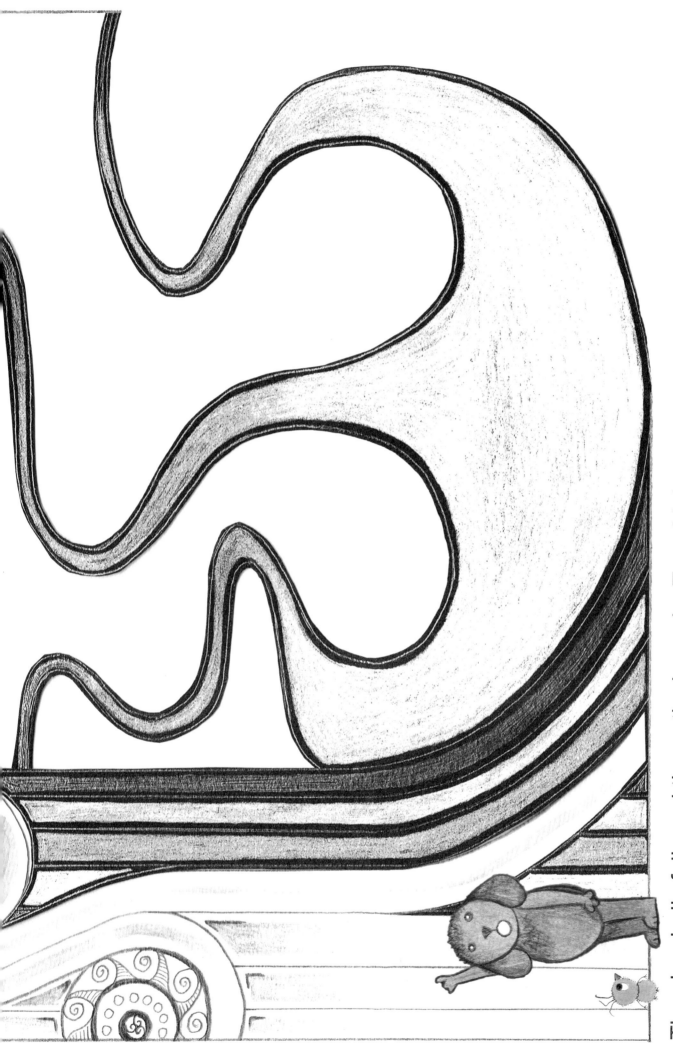

They hurriedly followed the path shown by Tane Mahuta.

Buddy and Chukpuk met the Maori Chief
who had tattoos all over his face.
"I know why you are here," he said. "Give
this manuka honey to your friend and she
will feel better. Now hurry, it's getting dark."

The friendly glow worms agreed to light the
way back to Peggy.

On their way, Buddy and Chukpuk heard
rustling in the bushes...

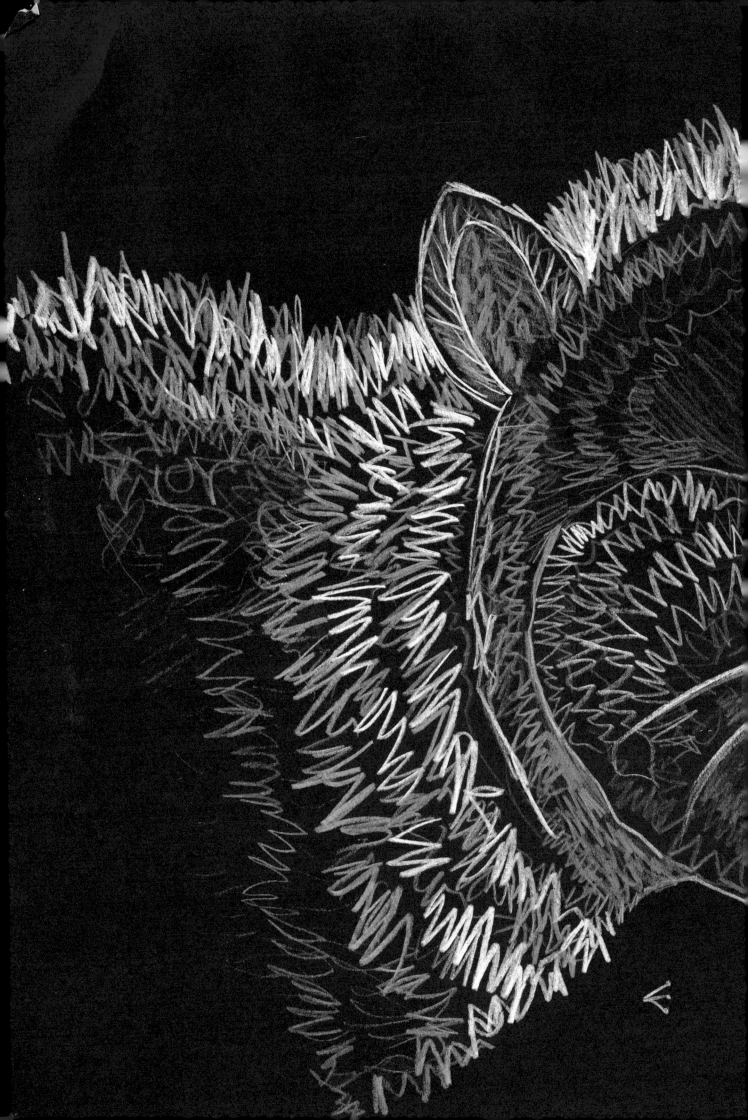

What's that noise?

KIWI KIWI

"Hey! It's a kiwi bird," said Buddy.

Kiwi hid behind Buddy.

"Phew! Thanks. That possum nearly caught me," said Kiwi.

At last, Kiwi, Buddy and Chukpuk found Peggy and gave her the healing honey.

Peggy whooshed up in the sky. She could fly again.
Yippee!

Kiwi celebrated by doing the Haka dance.

Buddy and Peggy were ready for their next adventure.
Kiwi would look after Chukpuk.

They waved goodbye as Buddy and Peggy soared into the sky.
They would never forget their New Zealand friends.

Ka kite ano!

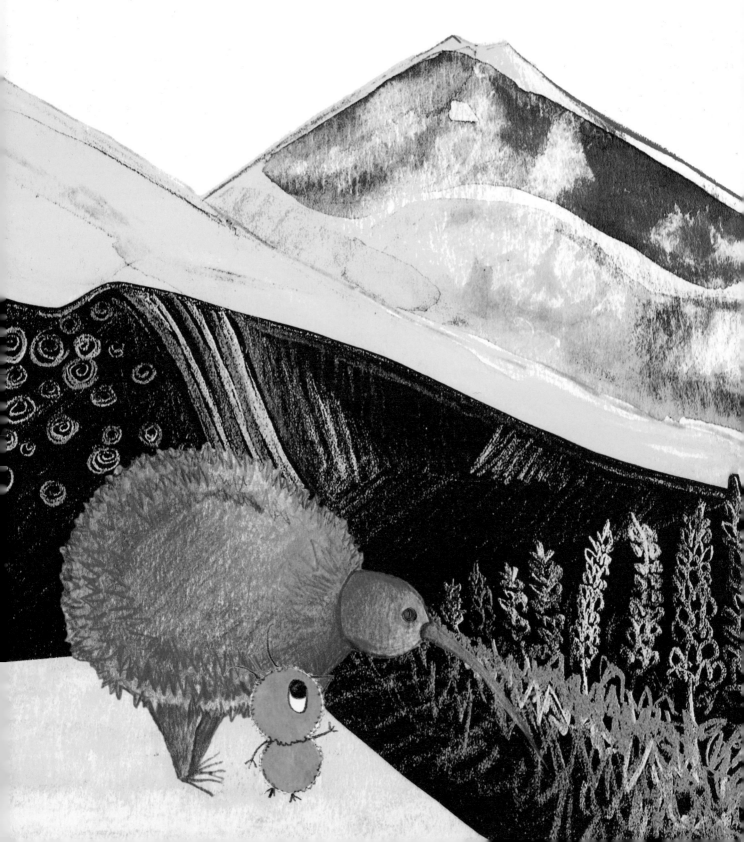